www.FlowerpotPress.com
CHC-0909-0466
ISBN: 978-1-4867-1584-8
Made in China/Fabriqué en Chine

Roar, Roar, Growl, Growl

Sounds from the Jungle

Written by Jennifer Shand
Illustrated by Barbara Vagnozzi

Did you hear that?

I hear **roar, roar, roar** and **growl, growl, growl!**

It's creeping along with a **grr**, **grr**, **grr** and a **scratch**, **scratch**, **scratch**!

What is that?

It's a tiger roaring and growling as he creeps along!

I hear ooo, ooo, eee, eee and aah, aah, aah!

They're swinging with a **whoosh, whoosh** and a **squeal, squeal, squeal!**

What is that?

It's a bunch of swinging monkeys whooshing through the trees!

I hear croak, croak, croak and grunt, grunt, grunt!

Ribbit, ribbit, ribbit with a hop, hop, hop!

What is that?

It's a frog croaking and ribbiting as she hop, hop, hops!

I hear **whistle,**
whistle,
whistle
and **squawk,**
squawk,
squawk!

Screech, screech, screech and talk, talk, talk!

What is that?

It's the talking
parrots screeching
and squawking!

I hear hiss, hiss, hiss and rattle, rattle, rattle!

It's moving with a **slither**, **slither**, **slither** and a **SSS, SSS, SSS!**

What is that?

It's a tropical rattlesnake
hissing and rattling as she
slithers all about!

I hear **chirp, chirp, chirp** and **click, click, click!**

There's a squeak, squeak, squeak walking all around with sticky, sticky feet!

What is that?

It's the gecko with sticky
feet chirping and clicking!

I hear roar, roar, roar and croak, croak, croak!

I hear whistle, whistle, hiss, hiss and chirp, chirp, chirp!

What is that?

It's a symphony of sounds from the jungle!

Wait...
Did you hear that?